Other titles in this series:
Barnaby's Cuckoo Clock
Tufty's Pot of Paint
Larry's Caravan

ISBN 0-86163-230-3

Copyright © 1988 Award Publications Limited
First published 1988
Fourth impression 1994

Published by Award Publications Limited,
1st Floor, Goodyear House,
52-56 Osnaburgh Street, London NW1 3NS

Printed in Singapore

FLIPPERTY'S AEROPLANE

Written and illustrated
by
RENE CLOKE

AWARD PUBLICATIONS
LONDON

No one thought that Flipperty Frog was
very clever so they all laughed when he said
he was going to make an aeroplane.

"You couldn't," jeered Tufty Squirrel.

"You wouldn't be able to make it fly,"
said Barnaby Bunny.

"What are you going to make it from," asked Bertha Bunny, "rushes and reeds from the river bank?"

"Just wait and see," said Flipperty. "One day you will see me flying over Hopping Wood."

He spent a long time hammering
and chopping away in his garden
and all the animals said how silly
he was.

Then one bright morning, just
after breakfast, they had the surprise
of their lives.

Sailing over the wood came a little red aeroplane.
Sitting in it was Flipperty Frog!

He waved to them and went flying away over
Hopping Wood Farm.

"He's done it!" gasped Dumpling, the black piglet.

"And it flies beautifully," said Merry, the kitten,
watching the aeroplane disappear in the distance.

"If he can make one,
so can we," said Larry,
the puppy. "Come on, let's
put our brains together."

They all thought very hard.
They nailed pieces of wood
together, they tied toy
balloons on to boxes, but
they could not make anything
that would fly.

Larry tried fastening an old
umbrella to a basket, then he climbed
on to the wall and sat in the basket.

"Now, Dumpling!" he cried. "Push me off and I'll open the umbrella."

Dumpling pushed and over went the basket. Although the puppy opened the umbrella, something went wrong.

The basket did not float gracefully across the farmyard but dropped with a bump on the ground.

"O—oh!" cried Larry, rubbing his head, "that wasn't much good."

Merry did not try any more.
She just went to sleep in the sun and dreamed that she was a beautiful butterfly with big, bright wings.

The next day Larry and Merry went along to Bertha Bunny's shop in Hopping Wood. All the animals were there and they were all talking about Flipperty.

"He came sailing over here yesterday," said Barnaby Bunny, "I nearly jumped out of my skin."

"I went down to the river to have a look at it," said Tufty Squirrel, "but he keeps it locked in a shed and no one can see inside."

"We asked Flipperty what made it fly," said Hazel Squirrel, "and he just laughed and said that was his secret."

"There's something mysterious about this," said Larry, "I'm going to find out what it is. I feel sure that Flipperty is playing some trick."

Larry walked along by the river the next morning.

Flipperty Frog was digging in his garden. There was no sign of the aeroplane but Larry saw that there was a new shed by Flipperty's house and he longed to see inside it.

"Are you going for a flight today?" he asked.
"Perhaps later on," answered the little frog.
"May I see your aeroplane?" asked Larry.
"Yes," said Flipperty, "when I fly over the
farmyard." And that was all he would say.

Larry went back to the farm and hatched a little plot.

"The next time I see Flipperty in his aeroplane I will rush down to his house and hide near by, then I shall see it land and have a good look at it."

That afternoon, Flipperty flew over the farm.

All the animals cheered but Larry slipped through the gate and ran down to the river.

He borrowed a ladder from Flipperty's garden and climbed into a tree.

"I'll pull the ladder up into the tree," he said to himself, "then it won't be seen."

Flipperty was having a long flight.
    Larry got very stiff and hungry sitting in
the tree and wished he had brought a bone to gnaw.
    At last he saw a speck appear in the distance —
yes, it was the red aeroplane!
    Larry peered through the branches as it came
near the ground.

Flop! it landed and out jumped Flipperty.
He lifted off the top half of his aeroplane
and out stepped a duck!
Larry gave a gasp of surprise, lost his balance
and toppled from the tree.

But he did not fall to the ground; a broken branch caught the back of his jersey and there he hung, in mid-air, while Flipperty looked up in amazement.

"Help!" shouted the puppy, "I'm caught. I can't get up or down!"

Flipperty thought it served him right but he was a kind little frog and did not say so.

"I'll fly over the farm and drop a message for help," he called to Larry.

Then he hopped back to the aeroplane, the obliging duck got inside again and Flipperty put on the top.

Off they went, over the trees to the farm.

"I hope they won't be long," gasped Larry.

"Here he comes again!" cried Dumpling as the red aeroplane appeared overhead. "And look, he's dropping something!"

Merry ran to pick up the message and she and Dumpling read it together.

BRING A LADDER TO THE RIVER BANK LARRY IS CAUGHT IN A TREE.

"Well, well!" said Merry. "That's what becomes of being inquisitive. Come along, Dumpling, we must go to the rescue."

They found a ladder and, taking an end each, they hurried off.

By the time they reached the river the aeroplane had been put away in the shed, but Larry still hung from the tree.

Dumpling held the ladder so that Larry's paws could reach it while Merry climbed the tree and unhooked his jersey.

The puppy was so stiff that he could hardly climb down the ladder but Flipperty was waiting at the bottom with cups of tea and buns for everyone.

"Thank you, Flipperty, for your help," cried Larry.

"And thank you for the tea!" cried the others.

Flipperty waved good-bye and hopped into his house.

Well, his secret was over, they would all be told about the duck inside his red aeroplane.

He felt rather cross, so he filled an extra cold water-bottle and put it in his bed to comfort himself.

But the next day Larry appeared.

"I've brought you a little flag for your aeroplane," he said. "I haven't told anyone about the duck and I won't."

They fastened the flag to the aeroplane, Flipperty was delighted and no one but Larry ever learned the secret of the flying frog.